Ruthie's Rude Friends

Jean and Claudio Marzollo

PICTURES BY

Susan Meddaugh

DIAL BOOKS FOR YOUNG READERS

E. P. Dutton, Inc.   NEW YORK

Dial easy-to-read

Published by
Dial Books for Young Readers
A Division of E. P. Dutton, Inc.
2 Park Avenue
New York, New York 10016

Published simultaneously in Canada by
Fitzhenry & Whiteside Limited, Toronto

Printed in Hong Kong by South China Printing Co.

The Dial Easy-to-Read logo is a trademark of
Dial Books for Young Readers
A division of E. P. Dutton, Inc. ® TM 1,162,718

Library of Congress Cataloging in Publication Data
Marzollo, Jean. Ruthie's rude friends.
Summary: Ruthie and her parents are the only Earthlings
on Planet X10 and she is very homesick until she meets
two creatures named Pig and Fish who help her escape
from a three-headed beast.
[1.Science Fiction.] I.Marzollo, Claudio.
II.Meddaugh, Susan, ill. III. Title
PZ7.M3688Ru 1984 [E] 84-1707
ISBN 0-8037-0115-2
ISBN 0-8037-0116-0 (lib. bdg.)

First Edition
COBE
10 9 8 7 6 5 4 3 2 1

The art for each picture consists of a drawing of pen
and ink and colored pencils, which is camera-separated
and reproduced in full color.

Reading Level 2.1

For Ruthie * *J. M. and C. M.*

For John and Justin * *S. M.*

Ruthie had been on Planet X10 for only two days.

And she was already homesick.

Dear Pam, she wrote

to her best friend on Earth:

The good thing about X10 is

it has less gravity than Earth.

That means I am lighter here.

I am so light that my hair

sticks straight out.

I can even jump over our spaceship!

The bad thing is

that the kids here make me feel shy.

I've seen three so far.

One has horns.

One has scales,

and one has sixteen eyes.

Their parents are scientists

like mine.

They have come from

all over the galaxy

to study this new planet.

9

I am the only kid from Earth.

It's AWFUL!

Love, Ruthie.

Ruthie put down her pen and sighed.

Now that she had finished her letter,

she did not know what to do.

Her parents were busy at the lab.

Finally Ruthie decided

to put on her word belt and go out.

"Stay inside the big wall,"
her mother had said.
"We don't know what lives
beyond the space station."
Ruthie walked over to the wall
and looked up at it.

"Click! Click!"

Ruthie jumped

when she heard the noise.

She turned and saw a strange creature.

It looked like a cross between
a flying fish and a butterfly.
"What in the world are YOU?"
she asked.
"Click, click," said the creature.
Ruthie switched on her word belt.
It turned the clicks into words.
"I'm a flutterfish," said the creature.
"But you can call me Fish for short.
Who are YOU?"
"I'm Ruthie from Earth," said Ruthie.
"You look very strange!" said Fish.
"Well, so do you," said Ruthie.
Another creature was coming over.

13

Ruthie laughed at him.

He looked like a small, fat child
with a pig's ears, hooves, and tail.
"That's Pig," said Fish.

Pig came over and laughed at Ruthie.
"Where did you get
those silly little ears?" he asked.

"They're better than yours,"
said Ruthie.

"How would you like
a punch in the nose?" asked Pig.

"How would you like
a knuckle sandwich?" asked Ruthie.

"Now, now, be nice," said Fish,
flying between them.

"Nice to an Earth girl?" asked Pig.

"Nice to a fat pig?" asked Ruthie.

Suddenly she noticed

that Pig was breathing faster

and getting fatter.

He began to float up in the air
over Ruthie's head.

"Hey, little Earth ears," he said.

"Bet you can't catch me!"

Ruthie jumped,

but Pig escaped her.

"You can't catch me!" he called.

Ruthie jumped and missed again.

She was getting mad.

Laughing, Pig flew by

and called her a skinny wimp.

Fish started laughing too.

Ruthie didn't know what to do.

She had NEVER been treated so rudely.

She hated Pig and Fish.

She ran away from them

as fast as she could.

As she ran

she thought about her ears.

"I may LOOK funny on X10,

but I know I'm BRAVE," she said.

"I bet there's something I could do
that Pig and Fish
wouldn't DARE do."
Ruthie saw the wall ahead of her.
A sign said, STAY INSIDE.
Ruthie jumped over the sign
and didn't look back.

Pig and Fish were watching her
with amazement.

"What are you DOING?" they cried.

Ruthie turned off her word belt
so she wouldn't hear them.

Slowly she started walking
away from the space station.
Soon she came to bushes
and then to pine trees.

Ruthie was scared,

but she tried not to show it.

After she had gone a long way,

Ruthie looked back.

She didn't see Pig and Fish.

She didn't even see

the space station!

Ruthie bit her lip

and realized she was lost.

Suddenly she heard something.

Ruthie froze.

Maybe if she stood still,

whatever it was would go away.

But the noise grew louder and closer.

Ruthie turned around
and saw Pig.
"Grunt, puff," he said.
Next to him was Fish.
"Click, click," said Fish.

Ruthie turned on her word belt.

"Did we scare you?" asked Pig.

"Not a bit," said Ruthie, lying.

"Were you lost?" asked Fish.

"Not at all," said Ruthie.

"I was just trying

to have a little PRIVACY."

Pig and Fish started laughing.

"How come you walk
and jump so much?" asked Pig.
"Don't you know how to FLY?"
Ruthie looked Pig right in his eyes.
"Of course, I know HOW to fly,"
she said.
"I just don't LIKE to fly.
I like to JUMP."
To prove her point
Ruthie did a few very fancy jumps.
"So?" said Pig.
"So, blow," said Ruthie.
"That's all you ever do, Tubbo.
You remind me of a balloon."

Pig looked a little hurt,

and Fish looked nervous.

"We're not supposed to be here,"

he said, looking around.

"Afraid?" asked Ruthie.

"Not me," said Fish.

Just then they heard
heavy footsteps in the forest.
"What's that?" asked Fish.

CLUMP! CLUMP!

The footsteps grew louder and
the air got hot.

Out of the pine trees
came a beast with three flaming heads.

The heads began to speak.

"Food for each of us!"
said one.

"Just in time for lunch,"
said another.

"Do you think they'll taste good?"
asked a third.

The heads licked their lips with fire.

"Let's get out of here!" yelled Fish.

33

He and Pig flew off.

Ruthie jumped after them.

"Wait!" she cried.

Pig and Fish looked down at her.

"Fly!" they cried.

"I can't!" she yelled.

The three-headed beast

was catching up with her.

SNAP!

One of the heads came close,

but Ruthie jumped away just in time.

SNAP! Another close call!

The heat from the flames was terrible.

Ruthie didn't know

how long she could keep jumping.

Just when she was about to drop,

she saw Pig and Fish

turn around in the sky.

Pig and Fish swooped down
and grabbed Ruthie.

SNAP! SNAP! SNAP!

The three heads almost got them all.

"Hang on!" yelled Fish.

"We'll try to keep you up!"

Ruthie held on

as tightly as she could.

But Pig and Fish could not
pull Ruthie through the air.
Together they began to fall.
Below, the three heads were waiting.
"Go on without me!" cried Ruthie.
"No!" said Fish.
Ruthie did not want
Fish and Pig to get hurt.
So she wriggled free and fell.

PLOP!

Ruthie landed near the beast,

rolled over,

and put her feet up.

When the first head came at her,

Ruthie pushed at it

with all her might.

As she did,

an amazing thing happened.

The head went spinning into the air

like a ball on a rubber string.

Another head

came at Ruthie.

She kicked this head, too,

and sent it flying.

"Hooray!" yelled Pig and Fish,

cheering from the sky.

"How did you do that?"

they cried.

"I'm not sure," she said.

"But it seems

that I'm stronger than they are.

Watch!"

The third head came for Ruthie.

BAM! She sent it spinning.

The three-headed beast howled
with all three heads
and ran back into the woods.

Pig and Fish landed.

"Can I feel your muscles?" asked Pig.

Ruthie held out her arm.

"WOW!" he said.

"You're stronger

than anyone on MY planet."

Ruthie was very proud of herself.

"I knew I could jump far here,
but I didn't know
how strong I was," she said.
"It's the difference in gravity.
My muscles are extra strong on X10."
Ruthie hugged Pig and Fish
and thanked them for helping her.
"I'm sorry about the way
I was acting," she said.
"I thought you were rude to me,
but the truth is that
I was rude to you too."
Pig laughed and said,
"We were all pretty mean."

Then Fish added softly,

"But things will be different now."

He flew up to Ruthie and gave her

a little flutterfly kiss on the cheek.

In her next letter to Pam
Ruthie sent a picture
of herself with Pig and Fish.
Underneath she wrote
in big round letters:
Planet X10 is much better
now that I have some friends.